The Rise of the Doppelgangers

Shahraan Sarfaraz Khan

It's the 1980s, and there's a town in Idaho that is quite abnormal. In that town lives a woman named Bessie. Bessie's house is the best-looking and most modern house in the town. The floor is made of marble, and the walls have geometric designs on them. Bessie throws parties every other day and invites the townsfolk to visit. They dress in their usual 1980s clothes: flannel coats and open t-shirts.

It's late at night, and Carl, an ordinary man in the town with a brown shaved beard and smooth skin, is playing ping pong. The party ends, and people spend the night at Bessie's house so everyone stays safe. Carl's wife is at their own home wearing a tan coat, with their daughter, who is only the height of a chair and wearing a long-sleeved shirt. They live in an old wooden house that is small, cold, and has holes in the floor.

Carl creeps up to the window and asks his daughter, "Can you please let me in?"

"But you told me not to open the door for anyone," replies the daughter. "Even you!"

"Just this time," says the father. The daughter thinks about it and eventually lets him in.

The mother quickly shouts, "STOP!" but it is too late. The daughter is torn in half and mauled by the doppelganger while the mother runs outside after seeing her daughter's lifeless body dragged into the other room. She runs through slippery puddles hidden in the grass before bumping into another doppelganger, which grabs her by the neck and eats her alive.

People are dressed in formal suits and dresses, and it is almost completely silent except for some cries and groans. It is cloudy with a bit of sunlight at noon. As someone buries each coffin in the moist, black dirt, distant rain can be heard. People who knew the mother and daughter come to the funeral, including Carl. When the funeral is over, Daryl sentences Carl to a small wooden box outside with no gem, which would have kept him safe from the doppelgangers, because he had kept their house gem in his pocket.

Later, as night approaches, Terry comes up to Carl and says, "I have an area for you to stay for the night that is safe," before handing him a gem. Carl goes to the safe place and stays there, but he cannot sleep because of the fear of being alone. He hears roars coming from outside the wooden cabin and shivers in fear as footsteps echo in the pale forest.

A family is going on a road trip for their daughter's 19th birthday while listening to the radio, which cancels out the noise of the ongoing thunderstorm.

"Will we make it?" says Angie, the older sister.

"We'll have to be careful on the road. Our tires might slip because of the water," replies Gary, the dad.

"Can you pass my Sprite™?" asks Bob, the little brother. As Angie grabs the Sprite™, it slips from her hands, spilling onto the map. Angie tries to grab the map to let it dry but ends up tearing it in the process. The family is left with no map, in the middle of nowhere, during a thunderstorm.

As everyone thinks it cannot get worse, their RV rolls over when one of the tires explodes. A table leg gets lodged in the little brother's leg. "AHHHH!" screams the boy as they look around for help while his leg bleeds heavily. Sally, the mother, spots a cabin in the distance, so they walk toward it. They find the cabin where Carl is staying and knock on the door. He answers, frightened, having forgotten it is morning, and is relieved to see the family.

"Where can we go to find help?" asks Sally.

Carl replies, "There's a town nearby across that road," pointing northeast. As they leave, Carl notices a flat tire and shouts, "But I can fix your tire!" Sally sighs in relief, and they head toward the town.

When they think they are lost, they finally find the town. Exhausted, they look around and see a man in a black suit staring at them. As soon as they blink, he disappears. Luckily, they find the survivor, Terry, and ask him for help.

"He needs help urgently!" says Sally. Terry rushes Bob into a small house equipped to treat injuries and carefully dislodges the table leg. Screams of pain echo across the town. Terry quickly wraps a bandage around Bob's whole leg before any more bleeding can occur.

Sally explains, "We were going on a road trip across Idaho for our daughter's 19th birthday, and then our tire exploded for some reason."

"There are a lot of thorns around the road here," replies Terry. The boy calms down a bit after the bandage is applied, and later they go to the diner in the town.

When they arrive, it's packed. Searching for a seat, they find out that the food is free. They take a seat, and to their surprise, the food is good for such a small wooden restaurant.

"Can we get four sandwiches with some fries?" says Gary.

Terry walks in and asks, "Mind if I sit?"

"Go ahead," says Gary.

Terry talks to all the family members in private except for Bob, for obvious reasons (the boy is six). The family doesn't take it seriously, but Terry reassures them that it's true. "If you don't believe me, ask someone else!"

Gary goes up to the waiter and asks, "Is it true that the doppelgangers are real?"

The waiter replies, “You must be new here. Take this gem. It’ll protect you from doppelgangers if you hang it on your wall. It’s true, but they only reveal themselves at night. The curfew is 6:20 because they start attacking as soon as the sun sets.”

The waiter notices it’s 6:23 p.m., so everyone else in the diner, along with the family, rushes out of the building to go to Bessie’s house. They bang on the door until they hear footsteps in the grass, fear in their eyes and their hearts beating like a massage gun. Bessie opens the door and says, “Come in!” They rush inside and close the door behind them, but they forget to lock it. As soon as Bessie reaches for the door handle, it’s shoved by countless zombie-like doppelgangers while everybody leans against the door to keep it closed. Bessie manages to lock the door before they make it in, but she is still scared to death.

After that, they do a head count. There were nine people before the family came in, so there should be thirteen. “Ten, eleven, twelve! We’re missing someone!” says Bessie. They notice Bessie’s cousin is missing. “Where’s Fred?”

They aren’t going to risk going outside for obvious reasons, so they stay the night. This is the family’s first time at Bessie’s, so they don’t know what to expect. In the morning, they put up posters and begin searching. If it were a normal person, they wouldn’t search, but Fred is a fast runner. They call and shout, but there's no response until they find him on a curb with his stomach slashed, alive but in terrible condition. They drag him onto the trailer of the truck they're driving and head back to town.

Back in town, the family is getting their new house from Terry.

"This old wooden house might not be the best, but it's the only extra we have," says Terry. As they explore the old wooden house, they discover a rusty locked chest. As they wonder what's inside, they see Terry and the town's nurse, Linda, carrying Fred on a stretcher. They are about to go upstairs when someone yells, "Fred must be dead!"

"They will come for us in the daylight if we keep him!" says a man outside.

"You're crazy!" replies someone else. The debate causes tension in the town. Terry comes up with some rules: if, within ten days, any doppelgangers come in daylight, Fred will be executed. If they don't, the man who started the debate will be executed.

The family is in Bessie's house during a party. Everybody's having fun, and it's the family's first time at a party. Gary plays cup pong when suddenly Sally hears a growling sound upstairs. They alert Bessie about the growling and grab a mop with a sharp handle since all the weapons are upstairs. They move slowly up the stairs, being extremely quiet so whatever is making the sound doesn't hear them.

They see the thing that's been growling. It's a doppelganger. Luckily, before it rushes at them, Bessie picks up a gun from a drawer. Bang! Bang! Bang! It's the most horrifying thing they've seen yet. "Party's over!" yells Bessie. Some people are disappointed, but most are relieved.

When everybody is asleep, the kid wakes up and walks to the kitchen. He grabs some crackers from the pantry, which he saw Bessie take during the party. But his dad stops him. "Why are you up?" says Gary.

"I can't sleep," says the kid.

They hear a sudden thud. One of the gems falls from the window, and then all of them fall to the floor. "Wake up!" Gary shouts. "Put the gems back!" Everyone hurries to replace the gems, but they forget one room: the basement.

A quick sigh of relief turns into a nightmare. Bessie suddenly remembers that the basement still has a gem on the ground and panics.

Sally says, "It's fine, I'll go get it."

Bessie quickly stops her and says, "The basement is known to be haunted and has a vent leading to the outside. Go get the small red lock in my bedroom." She rushes to the bedroom and grabs the lock. "This should block the demons for enough time."

In the morning, most people wake up, and the family decides to go to their house.

Angie says, “Why don’t we get to know the place a bit more?”

“That’s too dangerous,” says Sally. “We’ll have to go with Terry.”

The family walks up to Terry, who is currently writing down the days for the Fred debate.

“Can you take us on a tour of the town?” asks Angie.

“How about I take you guys to the park?” Terry says gladly. They walk steadily up to the rusty old swing set, thinking about what happened to this once-happy playground. Suddenly, they hear a growling and hissing noise coming from a nearby bush. It’s a raccoon. It jumps at them, scratching and clawing, so they run away, and one of them kicks it aside like a soccer ball. They end up running into a dangerous area filled with lethal animals.

“This might not be a good area to be in,” Terry exclaims.

“Why not?” asks scared little Bob.

“There are snakes, raccoons, and even crocodiles!”

Terry pulls out his compass and leads everyone to the southwest. They don't know that something has followed them on their way home.

The next morning, Terry is tallying the number of days on his notepad. It's day four of the Fred debate.

"I think we should end this debate early," Terry tells Daryl.

"Why?" asks Daryl.

"I think it's a waste of time," replies Terry.

Right before they start arguing, a crowd begins chanting, "Bring him down! Bring him down!" Apparently, someone has drained all the water in the well. There are three suspects: a man with short brown hair and a shaved beard, a girl with long blonde hair and hazel eyes, and the main suspect, a man with long curly brown hair and a thick, bushy beard.

"Why do you think he's the one who did it?" Terry yells at the crowd.

"Well, he was the closest one to the well at the time," a bystander explains.

Terry begins an investigation into who emptied the well. The only people who know how to drain the well are those who work for the town. The suspects are Terry, Daryl, Linda, and the waiter,

Jess. But whoever did it must have touched the wheel with their fingers.

Terry pulls out his pencil and notebook, puts the notebook back, and chips a piece of graphite off his pencil. He rubs it on the wheel that drains the well using his sleeve. Then he grabs a piece of tape from his office and sticks it on the graphite-covered wheel. Just like that, he finds the fingerprint of the culprit.

"You three, come to my office."

Terry lays down thirty little pieces of tape and some graphite powder. "Dip each of your fingers in the graphite and press each finger on one piece of tape." As they dip their fingers in graphite and press them on the tape, Terry notices a match to the fingerprint. The blonde woman, Kate, is the culprit.

"Why did you do it?" Terry yells.

"To stop them," whimpers Kate.

"Stop who?" he asks.

"The doppelgangers. They come from the well."

"Tell me more," Terry says, intrigued.

"I observe them every night. They climb out of the well. There must be a source where they spawn from," explains Kate.

"In the well?" Terry asks.

"I drained it so I could climb down and find where they come from," she explains.

"Are you sure? It seems very dangerous and unknown," warns Terry.

"It's our only chance of escaping, Terry."

"I'm sorry, but it's too risky," says Terry as he starts to leave.

Kate grabs Terry's hand and says, "Wait! Don't leave. I have a plan."

Kate explains her plan to Terry about how to escape, and it makes Terry start to believe her.

"So, when are you going to do this plan?" asks Terry.

"Tomorrow at 6 p.m. sharp," she answers.

At 6 p.m. sharp, everyone is locking their doors, putting up their gems, and closing their windows. Terry arrives in his spare suit, trying not to get his regular suit dirty.

"So, we enter by rope?" says Terry.

"Yes," replies Kate.

Terry stares at the faint orange glow at the bottom of the well, and his stomach tightens in fear.

Terry climbs down first, then Kate follows, but halfway down the rope, they hear a snip from above the well. Kate plummets to the floor, spraining her ankle. There is no second option, and they are trapped. They step into the glowing orange portal that leads to a dark, cold forest. As they walk around, they see something, an exact replica of their town. Every single person is the same, even Terry. They realize that the doppelgangers have been coming from this very town.

"If we kill all of them, we'll be free from the doppelgangers," whispered Terry.

"How do we do that?" asks Kate.

Terry pulls out two pocket knives, handing one to Kate. As Kate approaches the town, Terry quickly stops her.

"There are like a hundred of them, including us! You'll get killed in there," whispered Terry.

"Blending in and sneakily killing them is our best option," whispered Kate.

"We should kill ourselves first," suggested Terry.

Terry sneaks up to Terry (the doppelganger), who is in his office. He stabs his doppelganger in the back, hitting his liver, and covers his mouth. Then he shoves the body under the bed. He acts like a doppelganger, emotionless and professional like himself. He sees the real Kate on the other side of town and winks at her, signaling that he is real.

Something that isn't in the original town is a grandfather clock, which rings exactly at 6:45. The doppelgangers slowly walk toward the well they have, which also contains another portal. Terry and Kate both stay hidden in their houses.

"What do we do?" asks Kate.

"We should loot houses for guns. I already found mine, and I know Daryl has one."

Kate finds three guns, and Terry finds one.

"We should sleep. It'll restore our energy," says Terry.

"What if they come back?" asks Kate.

"I have an alarm clock in my house. We should sleep there," answers Terry.

At 5:00 a.m. in Terry's house and office, the alarm clock rings, and they panic and wake up. They have one hour to prepare for sunrise.

"We should wait until sunrise to attack. There's nothing else to do," says Kate.

"I'll do something in the time that we have," says Terry.

One hour later

"The sun is rising!" Terry yells.

They hear rustling noises from the well and load their guns. By the time the first doppelganger peeks its head from the well, bang! A clean shot to the head. One after another, they start coming out and getting shot until they think of something brilliant. Instead of one person climbing the rope, there would be three. As the first doppelgangers get popped, they struggle because of the speed and ammo of the guns. Even using dual pistols isn't fast enough for the horde of doppelgangers. They run toward Terry's house, blistering through the cold air. Terry locks the door as Kate panics. He holds Kate's hand and runs out the back door. As soon as he shuts it, the doppelgangers burst through the front door. They wreck the place, flipping tables and beds, looking everywhere for them. Terry brings her to a bush to hide, watching all the doppelgangers cramped into one house.

"3, 2, 1," counts Terry.

BOOM! All the doppelgangers blow up, or so they thought. Terry walks back, looking at his house in flames. He turns around as soon as he hears footsteps behind him.

"Hey, Daryl!" Terry says excitedly. "How are you doing?"

Daryl grabs a pitchfork from the ground and throws it at Terry. It misses him by an inch but hits Kate in the leg. Terry shoots him in the stomach, but Daryl barely reacts. He doesn't seem hurt, but Terry finds a way to take him down.

"Go in a house. I'll handle this," Terry tells Kate. Terry aims his gun at Daryl's eye, bang! He is blinded in one eye, which Terry takes advantage of. He gets closer from his blind spot, but Daryl turns his head. He grabs Terry and lifts him up, and suddenly Kate gets up and charges at him. She stabs the pitchfork into his hip, puncturing his lung and breaking his lower ribcage. Daryl starts limping, slowly edging toward the fire. Finally, when he gets close enough, Terry pushes him with full force. Daryl tips over, slowly burning in the flames.

As the sun fully rises, they head toward the well and climb down it. They take the rope too, since someone had cut it in the real world. They have just escaped what felt like a war but was really only thirty minutes. Terry throws the rope up and loops it around the nail at the top of the well, then climbs out. When he gets up, he announces the news about the doppelgangers. Everyone cheers, but there is still one problem—they are still trapped.

Terry has a plan to destroy the portal and free the townspeople. That night, every person is required to bring the most flammable and explosive materials they have to throw into the well. Terry plans to drop a match into it at exactly 7:00.

At 6:57, three minutes before the explosion, everyone happily throws their wood, gunpowder, and dynamite into the well. At 6:59, Daryl admits that he cut the rope for the well and apologizes.

"Why would you do it?" asks Terry.

"I found out Carl wasn't dead, but before I thought of killing him, he said you gave him a spot. So I saw what you were doing and cut the rope. But after I cut the rope, I felt guilty trying to stop you."

"It's okay," says Terry.

Ding, ding, ding! Terry lights the match and throws it into the well before everyone runs away from it. As it erupts like a volcano, everyone cheers and walks toward the road. After five minutes of walking, they see buildings and skyscrapers. They run happily to the city with a great sense of relief.

"We did it, Kate! We did it!"

Made in the USA
Coppell, TX
26 February 2026

72839744R00015